To the children reading this book-
Give your dreams wings, and watch them soar.
-AM

ISBN 978-1-304-67860-7

Text copyright© 2011 by Afiya T. Moore

Cover, Illustrations, and Layout by Bro. Boze

Jimmy Collar

and
His one and only Dollar

by
Afiya T. Moore
Illustrated by Bro. Boze

Jimmy Collar wished for just one dollar,
imagining all that he could do.
He thought out loud, chest puffed proud,
"Why, I could buy a toy car in blue."

"Or fifty gumdrops from my favorite penny store
and sugar candy canes, flavors galore,
with money leftover for an apple or two.
I could take my dollar to the petting zoo
and purchase food to feed the goats.
Or I could use my dollar to purchase a shiny red boat."
As Jimmy Collar's thoughts and wishes filled the air,
his mother overheard for she was always near.
She thought to herself, "If Jimmy Collar only truly knew,
there's so much more one dollar could do."
She called out to Jimmy Collar so tender and sweet,
"Come here little Jimmy for you have a treat."

Jimmy Collar got up with haste.
His mother gave great treats there was
no time to waste.
As he rushed in to see her,
the wish for his dollar had almost slipped his mind.
He held on to it one more time.

He wondered and wondered what could this treat be,
this was a surprise he couldn't wait to see!

His mother picked him up, gave him a hug and a kiss
and looked him straight in the eyes.
"I overheard your wishes, so this treat should
come as no surprise.

You are a very good boy, better than you realize."
"Here is your dollar to do with what you wish."
Jimmy Collar held his dollar up in the air in pure bliss.
He turned 'round and 'round and leaped for joy,
"My very own dollar! Oh, boy!"

He stuffed his dollar in his pocket.
Destination- toy store, off he went.
He remembered that blue toy car cost just fifty cents.

On the way to the store Jimmy Collar ran into
Mikey Avenue. Jimmy said,
"Hey there Mikey, what's wrong with you?"
Mikey Avenue had a very long face.
He was sobbing quietly, sitting still in one place.

Mikey Avenue lifted his head and said
with a tear leaving his eye,
"I had three quarters in my pocket
just enough to buy bread.
I must have lost one quarter on my
way to the store
since now I have two instead.
If I return home without a loaf of bread
in my hand,
I'll be in deep trouble with Mother and deep
trouble I can't stand."

Jimmy Collar
began to ponder about his one and only dollar.
"If I take my one dollar and make change as
four quarters and give one quarter to Mikey Avenue,
I'd have three quarters left and that's still enough
for my toy car in blue."

Jimmy Collar spoke to Mikey Avenue concerning his dollar,
"I have this one and only dollar that my mom
just gave to me,if I give you a quarter,
I will still have three."

"Come on Mikey, let's go to the store and get change.
Then you can buy your bread and be on your way."

Mikey Avenue's face lit up and his eyes were
bright as bulbs as he smiled.
They dashed to the store and were there after a while.

When they arrived at the store, Jimmy Collar
got change for his dollar and gave Mikey Avenue
a quarter just as he said.
Mikey Avenue thanked Jimmy Collar over and over
and left the store with his bread.
Jimmy felt great about being able to help his
friend in need.
His thoughts quickly went back to the
toy car in blue, he picked up speed.

He searched aisle after aisle, on the hunt
for the blue toy car.
He searched near and he searched far.

He passed up balls, scooters, skates and toy jets,
jump ropes, board games and train sets.

Just as he spotted the toy cars off
in the distance, he noticed Patty Pumpernickle
holding a doll hugging and kissing it.

Jimmy Collar
asked "Patty,
why is it you hug and kiss
the doll here in the store?
If you paid for her and took her
home you could love her even more."
"Well, Jimmy Collar," Patty Pumpernickle began to speak,
"I do not have enough money to buy the doll and take her home to keep.
I am saving money in my bank and I have almost all I need.
Just fifty more cents and she'll come home with me."

Fifty cents is the same as two quarters, which
Jimmy Collar did have.
Patty Pumpernickle only being able to love the doll
in the store was quite sad.
Jimmy Collar pondered in his head, "Well, if I give
her two quarters I will only have one.
On the bright side, that's enough for chewing gum."

With just one quarter he would not be able to
buy his car,
since he would be helping two of his friends so far.

"Here you are Patty Pumpernickle,
two quarters to purchase your doll and take her home.
I do not like the doll here in the store alone.
Take her home so she can be with you.
I know you will love her as I have seen you do."

"Oh thank you Jimmy Collar!"
Patty Pumpernickle exclaimed.
She rushed out of the store to go home
and collect the rest of what she had saved.
On her way out she called, "Thank you Jimmy,
I will never forget this day!"
"Awww....shucks," with a huge grin,
was all Jimmy could say.
Jimmy Collar was delighted to see
Patty Pumpernickle filled with so much joy.
He totally forgot about his blue toy car
as he began to search the store.

He went to the gum aisle searching for
his favorite flavor.
Raspberry Sugar Plum, was his favorite gum,
the one he loved to savor.

Jimmy Collar walked to the counter to stand
in line and purchase his chewing gum.
Bobby Wallabe was in line in front of him.
Bobby Wallabe had a hungry cat
at home that he had to feed.
Two cans of cat food are all he would need.

As Bobby Wallabe counted his change,
he noticed something strange.
Scratching his head and scrunching his nose,
he counted once more-
something strange he noticed just as before.

Bobby Wallabe needed a quarter to
buy food for his pet.
Jimmy Collar, who used to have a dollar,
had one quarter left.

He thought, "Today I helped Mikey Avenue buy bread
and a doll for Patty Pumpernickel,
but nothing for me.
If I give my last quarter to Bobby,
moneyless I'll be.
It's really important that Bobby has food for his cat.
Bobby Wallabe's not able to feed his pet,
I don't like the thought of that.
But I really, really wanted my
Raspberry Plum Chewing gum.
If I give up my quarter, I'll have none."

Jimmy Collar didn't have a clue.
What do you think Jimmy Collar should do?

Jimmy Collar with grief began to speak,
"Bobby Wallabe I have a quarter and it's yours to keep.
Now take this quarter because it's very important
that you feed your pet.
If I bought my gum and didn't give you the quarter
it would be a decision I'd regret."
"Thank you Jimmy Collar!
What a great friend you are!"
Bobby Wallabe purchased his pet
food and left the store.

Jimmy Collar walked home with no toy car in blue,
nor fifty gumdrops from his favorite penny store,
nor sugar candy canes, flavors galore,
nor money leftover for an apple or two.

He wouldn't be able to go to the petting zoo
to purchase food to feed the goats,
nor buy a shiny red boat.
He was a little sad and walked home
with his head hung low,
thinking, "I had my very own dollar and
now have nothing to show."

He thought a little deeper on all that he had done
and realized helping and giving was really, truly fun.
He began to smile as he thought of
Mikey Avenue and the bread,
he thought about how thankful his friends
were and the nice things they said.

He remembered Patty Pumpernickel
sadly hugging the doll in the store-
now the doll has a home where
Patty can love it even more.
He thought about Bobby Wallabe and his cats,
their stomachs full with food.
These thoughts put Jimmy Collar
in a very good mood.

He couldn't wait to get home to tell his mom
about how he had helped his friends.
Yes, the dollar was important,
but not more important than them.
"Mama, Mama, you'll never believe,
the dollar you gave me helped not
just one of my friends, but three!"

As Jimmy Collar began to tell his mom what he
had done,she could do nothing but smile.
This was her wish all the while-for Jimmy Collar,
to take his dollar and not just think of himself.
There are many people, just like his friends,
that need help.

"My little boy Jimmy, I am so very proud of you.
You've learned a valuable lesson about what just
one dollar can do."

His mother reached in her pocket and pulled
out a crisp five-dollar bill,
"Here's five more dollars to do with what you will."

Jimmy Collar was more than thrilled.
He could do the unimaginable with his
five-dollar bill!